This
Korky Paul
PICTURE BOOK
BELONGS TO:

_____

_____

Endpapers by Eve Bannister aged 9.
Thank you to St Ebbes CE Primary School, Oxford
for helping with the endpapers.
For my son Peter – R.T.
For Matina and Joanna – K.P.

OXFORD
UNIVERSITY PRESS

Great Clarendon Street, Oxford OX2 6DP
Oxford University Press is a department of the University of Oxford.
It furthers the University's objective of excellence in research, scholarship,
and education by publishing worldwide in

Oxford New York

Auckland Cape Town Dar es Salaam Hong Kong Karachi
Kuala Lumpur Madrid Melbourne Mexico City Nairobi
New Delhi Shanghai Taipei Toronto

With offices in

Argentina Austria Brazil Chile Czech Republic France Greece
Guatemala Hungary Italy Japan Poland Portugal Singapore
South Korea Switzerland Thailand Turkey Ukraine Vietnam

Oxford is a registered trade mark of Oxford University Press
in the UK and in certain other countries

First published 1993
First published in paperback 1995
Reissued with a new cover 2008

2 4 6 8 10 9 7 5 3

British Library Cataloguing in Publication Data
Data available

ISBN: 978-0-19-272711-4 (paperback)

Printed in China

Paper used in the production of this book is a natural,
recyclable product made from wood grown in sustainable forests.
The manufacturing process conforms to the environmental
regulations of the country of origin.

A Korky Paul Picture Book

Sanji and the Baker

Written by Robin Tzannes

OXFORD

UNIVERSITY PRESS

When Sanji was a young man,
he travelled a great deal.
He sailed across stormy seas.

FRATSIA

He travelled over hot, open deserts.

One day he arrived in the fabled
city of Fratsia, a dazzling place where
merchants traded in spices, gems,
and colourful silks.

Sanji decided to stay there a while.

He found a room that suited him
perfectly. It was small and simple
but quite cosy.

Best of all, it was right above
the Baker's shop.

In the morning Sanji awoke to a delicious smell wafting up from the bakery.

Dark, crusty bread hot from the oven.
Warm, sweet rolls filled with juicy currants.
Crunchy biscuits covered in sesame seeds.

Sanji stepped on to his balcony and
took a deep breath. He whiffed and
sniffed the heavenly aroma. Mmm . . .
fresh cinnamon buns.
He just had to have one.

In the bakery Sanji bought the tiniest cinnamon bun in the shop.
'I've been on my balcony enjoying the wonderful smells from your oven,' he told the Baker.
'Oh, you have, have you?' growled the Baker. He narrowed his eyes and glared at Sanji.

That evening when Sanji came home, he stood on his balcony to inhale the lovely smells that rose from the bakery.

Sweet coconut cakes and orange spice, date nut loaves and walnut whirls.

Sanji stood dreamily, sniffing and whiffing. He didn't see the Baker staring up at him.

This went on for many days.

Suddenly one evening the Baker banged angrily on Sanji's door. 'Thief!' he cried. 'You are stealing my smells!'

Sanji was astonished. 'What are you talking about?' he asked, opening the door.

'Don't think I haven't seen you, standing on your balcony whiffing and sniffing!' shouted the Baker. 'You smell my bread every morning. You smell my cakes every evening! I *must* be paid for those smells!'
'Nonsense!' said Sanji. 'Those smells come up here by themselves. I haven't stolen anything from you!'

The Baker shook his fist at Sanji. 'So you refuse to pay! Then I'll take you to court. The Judge will see that I get my payment!'

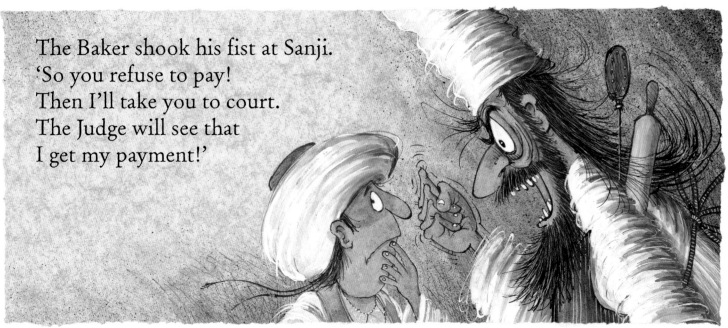

So they went to court.
The Baker told his story and
the Judge listened carefully.
Then he questioned Sanji.
'Do you enjoy those smells?'
'Yes, your Honour,' Sanji replied.
'And have you ever paid for them?'
'No, your Honour, I haven't.'
The Judge thought for a long time.

At last he said, 'Both of you will
return to court tomorrow morning
at nine o'clock. Sanji, you will
bring five silver coins.'

Sanji was miserable.
He didn't have five silver coins.

He would have to borrow
them from his friends.
And how would he ever
pay them back?

The next morning at nine o'clock
the Judge entered the court room.
Sanji stood quietly, with his
head bowed.
The Baker was there too, grinning
and rubbing his greedy hands
together.
The Judge spoke first to Sanji.
'Have you brought the silver coins?'
'Yes, your Honour,' he answered
in a whisper.

The Judge took a large copper bowl and placed it before him. He told Sanji to throw the coins, one at a time, into the bowl.

To the Baker he said, 'Now listen carefully . . .'

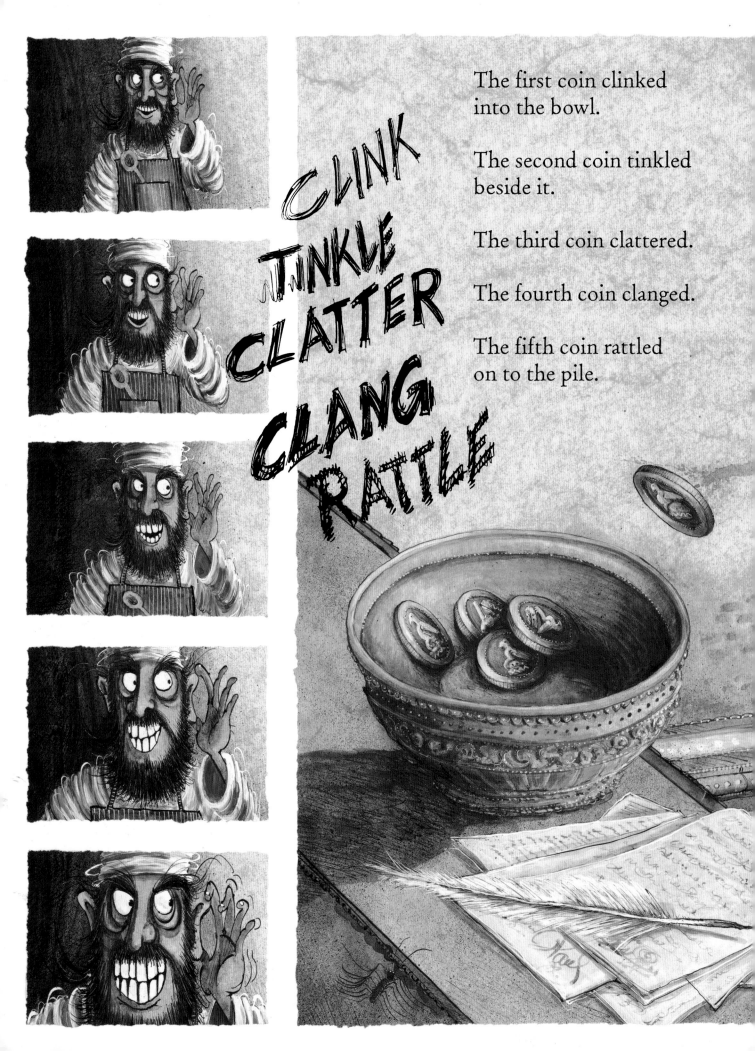

CLINK

TINKLE

CLATTER

CLANG

RATTLE

The first coin clinked
into the bowl.

The second coin tinkled
beside it.

The third coin clattered.

The fourth coin clanged.

The fifth coin rattled
on to the pile.

The Judge turned to the Baker.
'Did you hear those coins clatter and clink?'
'Yes, your Honour,' replied the Baker,
looking hungrily at the bowl of coins.
'And did you enjoy the sound of their rattle
and clang?' asked the Judge.
'Oh, yes! I certainly did!' cried the Baker.

'Good,' said the Judge. 'Because *that* was your payment.'

'And you, Sanji,' he continued,
'may have your five silver coins back.'
'Thank you, your Honour.'

www.korkypaul.com